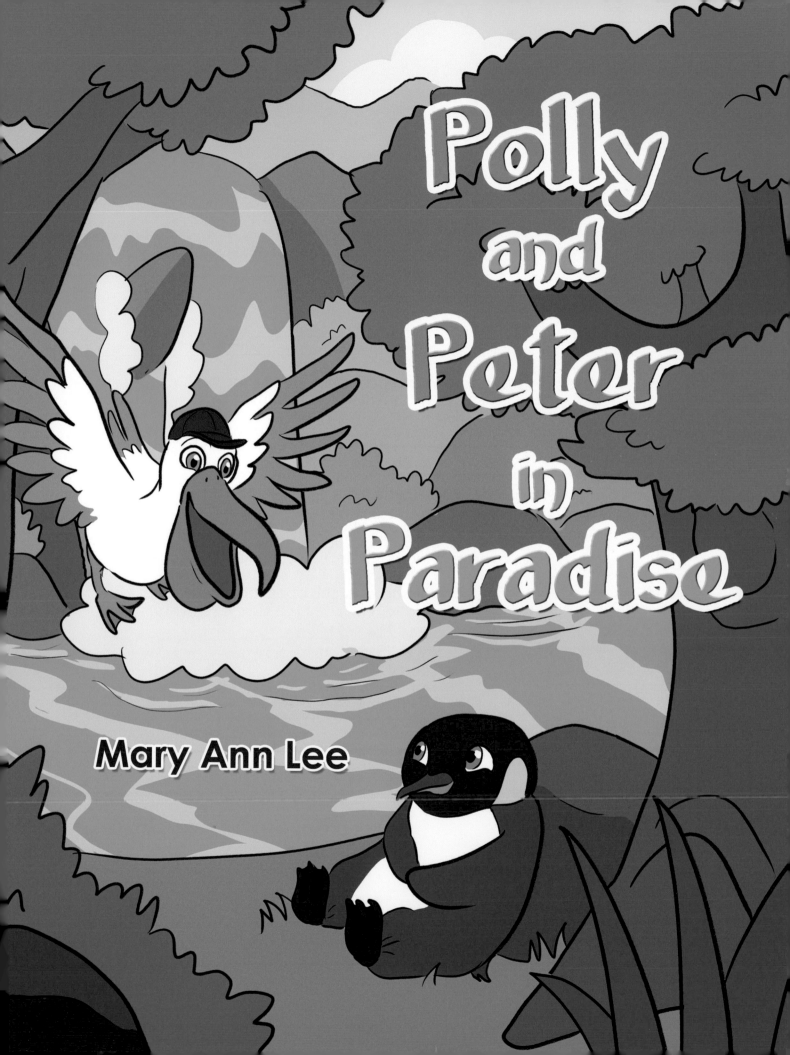

To order additional copies of this book, contact:
Xlibris
844-714-8691
www.Xlibris.com
Orders@Xlibris.com

ISBN: 978-1-6698-7311-2 (sc)
ISBN: 978-1-6698-7312-9 (e)

Print information available on the last page

Rev. date: 04/04/2023

Polly
and
Peter
in
Paradise

"Polly, Polly, you won't believe what I heard and what I saw! You won't! You won't!" "All right, all right, Peter," Polly's Pelican sidekick, said. "Calm down! You better not be exaggerating again. We are all fed up with your outlandish stories." Polly, an exceptionally intelligent king penguin, the unofficial leader of their little band, spoke for all of them. "So now that you have awakened us from our delightful afternoon nap, tell us succinctly what you observed."

Oscar, an incredibly wise owl, becoming agitated, determined it was time to intervene. "Peter, you have our full attention which we all recognize you relish. Tell us why you have caused all this commotion." "Yeah, come on, Peter, we are on pins and needles, whoops, not mine of course, waiting to hear your tall tale." Prissy, the resident porcupine chimed in. Assured that he had everyone's attention, Peter began to speak with an unsteady voice.

"Friends, I saw and heard a frightening encounter between Adam, Eve, and our Creator, God himself."

Everyone could sense the tension in Peter's voice as he began to tell them what he had seen. It was going to be life changing for each of them; he must select his words carefully. As he often did, he wished Polly were standing right beside him instead of at the back of the group. She was much more articulate than he; more importantly, everyone believed her. "Oh, if only I had not made up so many stories in the past, they would believe me now, "he silently reprimanded himself.

"We all know how Adam and Eve enjoyed walking in the garden with God in the coolness of the day as they marveled at His creation. Today, however, was an exception. Something I just happened to observe and overhear was very disturbing."

The entire group immediately turned to focus on Peter. What could he have seen that would have been so disturbing? After all, this was God's unspoiled garden! Everything about it was flawless; their perfect Creator had made this garden for all of them. In addition, God had told Adam that he was to oversee the caring for and the naming of the animals, which had been an exciting time for all of them. Adam instructed all of them to line up in single file and patiently wait their turn as he determined by what name they would be called. After deliberate thought and examination of each animal, sometimes seeking Eve's opinion, he began the process based on their defining features. Adam thoroughly enjoyed this process so much so that he determined to not only name their species, but at the urging of Eve, he also gave them a personal name.

When Winston, a huge, whimsical walrus received his name, he blurted out in his baritone voice: "My name suites me perfectly because although it sounds regal; everyone knows I'm the life of the party." A sweet blue fox in the group Forrest spoke up quietly, agreeing that Winston was aptly named. "I do not understand my name; however, it seems rather majestic for a creature as small as I." "On the contrary, Forrest," Sage, a quiet little sparrow, interjected, "your name suites you well because you know everything that goes on in the forest, and you care about everyone who lives in it. I think we should call you Faithful Forrest. Adam dearly loves you because you are so kind."

Cheers went up throughout the small group of friends, showing that they all agreed about that description of Forrest. Emma, an exceptionally large elephant, thought her name suited her image of being much smaller than her actual size. Track, a dawdling tortoise and his side kick Sally, a friendly, silly skunk, never gave their names any thought. "Excuse me everyone, I do believe we are all gathered together to listen to a curious tale from our pattering friend Peter," said Oscar, who was easily agitated

When time was wasted, especially when he could be napping, urged Peter to continue his story. "Please, make it brief, for once," Lance, a truly cowardly lion, chimed in, adding a huge yawn to emphasis his boredom. Peter realizing it was time to speak or lose everyone's attention, stretched up as tall as he could, trying to appear trustworthy. He began his story. "Yesterday afternoon, as I was preparing to dive into the cool water, I heard God calling out for Adam. He wanted to know where he was. Adam, who had always been eager to talk with God, was now hiding in fear. He was hiding from God!"

Upon hearing this startling news, the animals began to banter among themselves. Track, looking around to make sure Sally was still close by, whispered to her; "This is an amazing accusation if true. Why would anyone hide from our loving God?" Sally, who adored him, looked up to Track in quiet disbelief. "Don't worry, Sally," he responded. "There must be more to the story."

As if on cue, Peter picked up his narrative. "As I was saying, Adam was hiding from God, so God…" Emma, with illusions of being petite, even though she was a massive elephant, blurted out; "What did Adam say? Oh my, what did he say to God about hiding? I do not understand why he would hide in the first place." Peter went on to explain that before Adam could answer, God spoke: "Adam, have you been eating of the forbidden tree?"

Upon hearing that, the little group of friends began expressing their confusion about the incident. Gregory, a magnificently spotted giraffe, spoke softly to his best friend Lexie, a very social Lama, to reassure her that all would be well. "Lexie do not be distraught; everything will be fine just as at the beginning. God has a plan, and He is incredibly wise, so we must trust Him." I want to believe you, Gregory, I really do, but this sounds serious. I am afraid."

Winston decided it was time to speak up. "We shall find the underlying cause of this. It may take time, but we will find out exactly what transpired along with the ramifications for each of us." He loved to throw in words like *ramifications* occasionally to impress this quaint band of friends.

The group was becoming nervous waiting for the rest of the story. They just could not comprehend why Adam would want to hide from their kind and loving God. As they were pondering the situation, Peter, once again, requested their attention. "Obviously, there is more to this story which I am eager to share with you. You see, friends, Adam hid from God because he and Eve had disobeyed God's command."

Lexie, nudged Gregory, indicating he did not know what Peter was talking about. Gregory was not sure he understood the whole story either but wanted to ease his young friend's mind. "Be patient a little while longer, and I'm certain we will be given all the details," he told his frightened little friend.

Lexie, who never liked to wait but did trust his good friend, responded determinedly: "I'll be good, Gregory; I won't get frustrated; I want you to be proud of me!"

Peter realized that he must continue with his story. "Friends, I need you to listen carefully to the rest of my story because it has ramifications for all of us." Winston's ears perked up at the use of such an impressive word spoken by Peter, whom he thought was not particularly bright. The rest of the little animal band were not sure they wanted to hear any more of Peter's story. It sounded so ominous. Lance, who seldom spoke, finally motioned for Peter to finish the story.

"After God found Adam and Eve hiding, they admitted that they had eaten of the forbidden tree. But they each blamed it on others rather than admitting to their disobedience." Peter continued.

Prissy jumped in; "Do you mean they really blamed each other?" Peter was not sure how to answer this without causing the group to be sorely disappointed in Adam, but they had to hear the rest of the story. "Adam, when confronted by God, blamed Eve for giving him the fruit. "That doesn't sound like our Adam," Emma interjected. Each of the animals nodded in agreement.

"It did not sound like him at all," Forrest, who almost never gave an opinion, quietly moaned. Olivia, a soft-spoken otter, and Forrest's' best friend, sighed in agreement.

Oscar, again wanting Peter to continue, jumped in asking the group to be silent and listen for the end of the tall tale. "We all agree that this action seems to us out of character for our kindhearted Adam. But let us hear what more Peter must share, which I feel certain will not be encouraging news." With that Polly turned to Peter and said, "Continue." Knowing what else he had to share would upset them, he took a deep breath and continued. "As I explained, each of them blamed someone else, not themselves. Eve dared to tell God that the serpent, which he made, had tricked her.

"Oh, that evil Serpent, who thinks he is so beautiful, always frightened me!" Track who had been silent until now, suddenly blurted out showing his reaction. "He always displays an arrogance, as though he thought he could be God." Emma interjected, "How foolish of him to ever think he would be anything like our God." "No one is as loving, kind, and wise as the Creator. We all recognize that." Prissy bristled adding that, she too, was frightened by that evil serpent and distraught at this news.

Polly then encouraged Peter to continue before there was too much commotion. "Oh, you should have seen the look on their faces when God confronted them. He told they were being expelled from the garden." Peter spoke with intensity. "Even watching this from my perch in the tree, I could see the disbelief and fear in their eyes. And since they must leave the garden, we must also leave. Polly, what are we going to do now?"

As she contemplated an answer for her comrades, she silently sighed at the burden she felt. "This is quite a dilemma we face. You are right Peter; we must leave with Adam and Eve. Oscar, as the wisest one in our group, I will need your help to organize our move out of the garden."

"Yes, yes, of course, Polly, As the wisest among us I will be pleased to help you organize out trek out of Eden. You and I should speak privately as we determine the best plan for our departure." "Peter, you need to lead the group over to that grove of trees nearby and wait until we come back to you with instructions. Can you do that, Peter, without causing anyone to panic?"

Peter felt flattered that Polly had asked him to watch over the group. He always wanted her to be proud of him especially since he frequently did foolish things for which they all paid the price. This time he would prove to her that he could be trusted. "Polly, he spoke with sincerity, I will not let you down, I promise." Polly then directed the group to follow Peter.

Once she saw her band of friends were out of sight, she looked at Oscar, hoping for encouragement. "Polly, we need a tactical plan if we are to quickly find a new home, which is not an easy task. Each member of the group must use his size and abilities if we are to achieve success. Polly, I will support your decisions."

"Thank you, Oscar, I will need your wisdom to initiate a plan that can be methodically explained to them. Lance, although he will not enjoy it, must provide leadership. He can look and sound ferocious if necessary; and with a little prodding, I believe I can persuade him to rise to the occasion. Biscuit, a playful bobcat, can join him, and she will love mimicking her dear friend."

Polly paused as she pondered the thought of a new place to call home, but they must get there first. Polly and Oscar resumed their task of assigning duties to each member based on their size and abilities. "Prissy could also be threatening if she used her quills effectively. Olivia and Forest, both shy and gentle, could stay undercover scurrying though the forest looking for danger. Olivia could smell water a long way off which would be vital."

Oscar noted that Emma, regardless of her desire to be petite would be able to forge a way forward along with Lance and Gregory, whose height would be invaluable for viewing the layout. "We have a good plan to leave the garden. Polly, don't you agree?"

As Polly nodded in agreement with their plan, she felt herself choke up at the thought of leaving paradise. None of them had any idea what lay outside the boundaries of the only home they had ever known. Pull yourself together, Polly told herself. As the leader, you cannot fall apart, or all is lost. Oscar, in his wisdom recognized what she was feeling; and in an uncharacteristic demonstration of affection, gently patted her head and reassured her all would be well.

Time was short; they had to organize the group quickly.

"Oscar, how can we manage to keep Winston in check? He must be serious with no joking around. Since Track does not move quickly, he would be good to pair up with him although when he chooses to, Winston can move surprisingly fast. Don't you agree?" "Yes, yes, of course, that is sensible," agreed Oscar. "Naturally, Sally must go with Track; she can ride on his shell."

"Oh, my, she will love that!" Polly responded to that suggestion.

Thinking to herself, Polly wondered if they had left out anyone. "Sage!" she blurted out to Oscar. "How could we have left out our sweet singing, Sage?" Polly was relieved that Sage would not know they had momentarily forgotten her. Oscar was quick to point out that although she was incredibly quiet and never drew attention to herself, she would have an extremely key role on their journey. Her ability to soar above the entire group, seeing any danger that may lie ahead would be vital. Polly and Oscar agreed they had a viable plan. Now, they have must decide the roles each of them would play. Oscar naturally would join in flying reconnaissance with Sage although he could not fly as quickly as she; but his size and wisdom, he thought to himself, would offer protection.

Before Polly could speak up to express what she felt she should do, Oscar spoke calmly to her. "Polly, you as the leader of our little group, and a very competent one I might add, must be visible to the entire group. Therefore, you must lead us out of the garden. Peter needs to go with you, or he will panic. The two of you could ride one on top of Lance and the other on top of Emma. You could be seen by everyone, and you could keep your eyes on the group." Of course, the problem was putting Polly on top of either one of the animals since she could not fly.

As Polly contemplated this obstacle, along with their daring journey out of the security of the garden, she began to feel the responsibility facing her. "Oscar, do you think you could find Adam and Eve. I would certainly be more comfortable if we could follow them. Do you agree?"

For a moment Oscar began to stumble for words, and then said in his forceful manner, "Polly, what a brilliant idea, and Adam would be pleased to see us. He must be worried about us because he does love us. I will fly off now and find him and deliver the news that we are going with them."

"Hurry, you must hurry, Oscar before it's too late." As Polly watched him fly up into the clouds, she realized she needed to return to Peter and the group. What would she find when she returned? No time to wonder now; she headed straight to the area in which she had left them. When Peter saw her, he yelled out to welcome her. He also wasted no time in telling her he had acted responsibly. Everyone was eager to her hear what she had to tell them. Peter asked them to quit chattering and let Polly speak. "Thank you, Peter, for keeping everyone calm, I am proud of you." Peter could not help but feel himself puff up a little at her complement. "We have a very important mission, and we cannot dawdle." "The only one that dawdles is Track or maybe Winston when he is being stubborn." Gregory blurted out jokingly.

Everyone but Track and Winston laughed until Polly spoke in a sharp tone. "All of you must listen carefully, as these plans must be followed exactly for our safety. Each of you has a significant role to play in this move out of the garden," Polly began.

But at that moment, Oscar flew into the group. "Excuse me, Polly, but I must interrupt. I went as you asked to find Adam and Eve, but they were rushing out of the garden. I spoke to Adam, and he glanced back at me with a remorseful look. Then it looked like he motioned for me to follow them. At that moment I realized we had to move right now or never find them in this new place we are headed. So carefully follow Polly's instructions."

"Lance, Biscuit and Emma you are the leaders; the rest of you take the positions we assign you. Prissy, remember who you follow. Forrest and Olivia, please be extremely cautious as you head out from us. Winston, you keep encouraging Track to move as fast as possible." Winston pondering this advice began to chuckle, but quickly realized this was not the time to joke around. He knew this was a serious moment. "Of course, Polly, I will fulfill my duty." Oscar scanned the group to find Sage. He felt she look frightened, so he spoke softly to her. "You can fly faster and longer than I, Sage; and considering my size and strength, we will make a good team. I will protect you; I promise." Sage felt less fearful now and was ready to begin her flight.

In her position atop Lance, (Lance had lain down so she could climb on his back) Polly surveyed her company of friends and assured each was in their assigned position, spoke to them. "Dear friends, this is a tough time for each of us, but we must trust our God who made us and placed us in the garden paradise. He will care of us now. We will find a pleasant home with Adam and Eve outside this garden, but we must always remember we are friends regardless of what lies ahead." With that said the group cheered and applauded Polly promising to always stay friends. Even though none of them could imagine anything else. Why would they not always be friends?

Polly's voice interpreted their chatter and gave a command to Lance to begin leading the caravan out of paradise. At her voice, the caravan slowly began making the trek out of the garden. Just before they took their last step into the new, unknown land they would call home, Polly scanned her remarkable group. She felt a sense of pride as she watched them carefully follow their leaders. One last word of instructions was necessary, she felt. So, from her perch on top of Lance, she said, "You are doing so well, and I am proud of you, but one word of caution. Do not under any circumstance look back. Keep your eyes ahead of you. Once we are outside of the garden, we will determine what must be done next.

"Lance was enjoying his role as a leader holding his head high, looking over at Emma occasionally nodding approval to encourage her when suddenly, a loud noise pierced the air. The entire entourage craned their necks to see what the commotion was.

Gregory had failed to notice an extremely high branch on a tree right in front of him and cracked his head on it. Sheepishly, he looked around at his companions and nodded to them apologizing for frightening them. "I will be more vigilant as we continue our journey, my friends," he assured them. "On we go now."

But before the band of friends took another step, Forest let out a shriek! "What in the world happened?" Olivia asked her friend. "I am not sure, but my paw hurts, and there is something in it." Olivia carefully examined his paw; then she called for Polly to look at it.

"Oh, yes, I am afraid there is something in your paw. Peter, come here and see if you can pull this out of his paw" After looking carefully at Forrest's paw, Peter determined he could pull out the invading object with his strong beak. One quick jerk and he had it. "Forest, I have it; I have it. How do you feel? Is your paw sore?" "Just a little," he responded. "Thank you so much, Peter. You are a good friend."

The group continued the journey sharing among themselves both concerns and expectations about their new home. As Emma and Lance stepped out of a thicket of shrubs, grasses, and tress and into an open meadow, Emma squealed: "Look, look, do you see what I do? This is amazing!" Lance let out a roar of excitement. Peter flew over to perch himself back on Emma's head to see what had caused the excitement. When he glanced around taking in the view that lay before him, he understood why she was animated. Indeed, this was beautiful territory stretching out before them.

Polly instinctively knew, however, that this beauty was deceiving and decided it was time to provide instructions and a warning to this little band of travelers.

"Could I please have everyone's attention so that we can discuss what our next move will be."

Because there was so much chatter going on, they did not hear her, so she determined it was time to use her voice of authority. She also decided she needed to be on Emma's back so that everyone could see her. Just as she was contemplating how to achieve that, she felt something slither through the grass passing right in front of her. Her instincts were right, the serpent was watching them; she had to act quickly. They were in danger! She had to alert them to his presence. The thorn in Forest's paw and Gregory hitting his head were just a foreshowing of the things to come. Evil had invaded their world just as it had Adam and Eve's. God alone knew what would happen to them, but she would do all she could to save them. They needed a savoir; she would be that for them. "Please God, my creator, do not let me fail. You love them, and so do I" she prayed.

The weight of this responsibility weighed heavily on her, even though she was a king penguin, she was petite in comparison to the others in this strange group. She was, however, determined to take them to safety. No more time to feel sorry for herself; she had to share the news that the Serpent was lurking about to harm them. They would have to be vigilant.

"Lance, please lie down so that I can climb on your back and then I can jump on Emma's back." For once, Emma was pleased to be big enough to assist her group of friends. Peter flew over to see what was happening and saw Polly perched on Emma's back. Peter, spoke with a clear voice, "Friends, our fearless leader needs everyone's undivided attention." He smiled at his best friend and nodded, encouraging her to speak.

"Each one of you is special to me and special to each other. You have demonstrated that over and over. You are also, more importantly, especially to God, our creator. We must understand that evil has crept into our world. Satan, the mortal enemy of God, and, therefore, enemy to all His creation, is on the prowl. As I was contemplating what I would say to you, he slithered past me in the grass making his presence known just enough to startle me, which he did. Now listen carefully each one of you. This enemy is an expert in deceit; he is a liar; he is angry at God for expelling him from heaven and now the garden. You must believe that he will stop at nothing to destroy God's highest creation, man, just as he did with Adam and Eve. You must always be alert to his deception for he will never stop until he draws you into his snare. Now, we must follow a carefully crafted plan if we are to survive. Each of us must look out for the entire group. Selfishness and arguments will only aid the serpent in his desire to create chaos among us. Divisions, putting yourself first, and listening to his lies will ensure that we fail to reach this new land. Satan will have won. Listen intently for the directions you are going to be given. No one is excused from following all directions without arguments. Time is not on our side. We must be vigilant, move quickly, and listen to all instructions. You have proved to be a vigorous and resilient band of friends. Now we must move forward but be alert to anything unusual"

A lump formed in Polly's throat as she motioned for this unique band of friends to strike out to find a new home, not another paradise. Polly, Peter and, certainly, Oscar, understood what lay ahead would bring about dramatic changes in their lives, most not pleasant. Their new world, like Adam and Eve's was now infested not only with thorns and bristles, but also with more deadly ills like envy, deceit, and hatred. How had it come to this? Somehow Polly understood that it was due to man's disobedience. Collectively, animals, and man, would suffer because of this affront to a Holy God. Surely, there was a solution.

Peter had overhead something else in the garden that offered hope. Without hope they would all perish. "Snap out of it!" Polly heard Oscar admonish her. "You cannot give in to mundane thoughts as we must hurry along. "Right! Right, you are Oscar! I apologize for my lack of focus. I am ready to move forward." "Polly," he gently said, "it will be all right. I promise; it will be all right." "Yes, of course, it will be. Here we go!" But in her heart, she knew that Oscar could not fulfill that promise. "God, you are the only salvation we have. Help us," she silently prayed.

Once her friends were safely out of the garden, she dared look back for one more glimpse of what had been Paradise. She swallowed hard trying to hold back her tears as she saw an angel with a flaming sword standing guard at the garden's entrance. No one, man or animal would ever enter Paradise again. Becoming overwhelmed with emotion, she sought out Peter. He may be less clever than Oscar, more tiresome than dawdling Track and even more unreliable than either Emma or Winston, but he was her best and most trusted friend. Yes, she must talk to Peter. Surely, he knows something that will provide her answers.

Peter, being Peter, was acting silly and trying to entertain the entourage when she came rushing up to him. But, Peter, the faithful friend that he was, recognized her despair, and immediately asked her, "What is troubling you, Polly? What has happened to make you distraught? None will escape my anger if they have hurt you"

"No, Peter, no one has hurt me, but I am distraught. She then recounted to him seeing the angel guarding the entrance to Paradise. Then, Peter, sighed, shook his head, and with distress in his voice shared with his special friend what else had transpired that fateful day in the garden. "Polly, I was so anxious, due to what I had heard in the garden and knowing what you must immediately hear it, in my haste I failed to finish the story. I am so sorry because that part is vitally important. If I understand what else God told Adam and Eve, we might still have hope."

"Tell, me Peter; do not keep me in suspense. Especially, if there is a glimmer of hope."

"More than a glimmer, I think, Polly, more than a glimmer! God promised, or it seemed so to me that He promised that He would provide a savior for Adam and Eve's offspring. Like you are for our little group, a savior to rescue humanity. Although this paradise is lost forever to man, a new one is being prepared; it will be perfect and eternal.

Polly, I believe in my feeble brain that I understand God has a grand plan. However, He gave no specific timeline or exact plan, Polly; I do so hope this gives you peace."

Polly looked intently at this unusual friend and nodded her head. "Hope, Peter; hope is the key word; without which we are doomed forever. I will cling to that. We animals recognize our creator can be trusted, hopefully, soon Adam, Eve and all their children will learn that, too. It is sad that we animals raise our voices, with so many different sounds to praise Him, but the humans do not seem to do that. They do not depend on Him as we do." "Peter, we cannot delay our journey as time is of the utmost importance. We must move forward on this adventure of ours outside the garden

Printed in the United States
by Baker & Taylor Publisher Services